**This Little Tiger
book belongs to:**

_____

_____

LITTLE TIGER PRESS LTD,
an imprint of the Little Tiger Group
1 Coda Studios, 189 Munster Road, London SW6 6AW
Imported into the EEA by Penguin Random House Ireland,
Morrison Chambers, 32 Nassau Street, Dublin D02 YH68
www.littletiger.co.uk
First published in Great Britain 2022
Text by Danielle McLean
Printed in China • LTP/2700/4365/1021
2 4 6 8 10 9 7 5 3 1

CRAZY STICKERS

CREATE-A-SUPERHERO

LITTLE TIGER

LONDON

SUPERFOOD

Let your imagination run wild and have a super-duper time! Add masks, capes, eyes, mouths, and more to make your very own superhero friends.

LET'S MAKE MUSIC

I like the sound of that!

SOLE MATES

FLYING HIGH

It's my time to shine!

Collect them all!

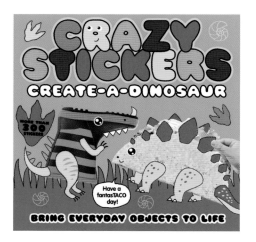

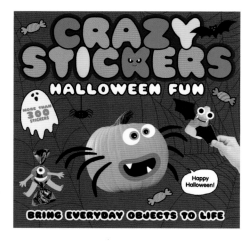